Kyle + Ali Machado

The editors would like to thank
BARBARA KIEFER, Ph.D., Associate Professor of Reading and Literature,
Teacher's College, Columbia University, and
ROBERT ASHER of the Doctoral Program in Anthropological Sciences,
State University of New York, Stony Brook,
for their assistance in the preparation of this book.

www.randomhouse.com/seussville

Library of Congress Cataloging-in-Publication Data
Worth, Bonnie.
Oh say can you say di-no-saur? / by Bonnie Worth.   p.   cm. —
(The Cat in the Hat's learning library)
SUMMARY: Dr. Seuss's Cat in the Hat shows Sally and Dick how dinosaur fossils
are excavated, assembled, and displayed in a museum.
ISBN 0-679-89114-5 (trade). — ISBN 0-679-99114-X (lib. bdg.)
1. Dinosaurs—Juvenile literature. [1. Dinosaurs.] I. Title. II. Series.
QE862.D5W67   1998   567.9—dc21   97-52314

Printed in the United States of America   10 9 8

Oh Say can you Say Di-no-saur?

by
Bonnie
Worth

illustrated
by
Steve
Haefele

The Cat in the Hat's Learning Library™

Random House 🏠 New York

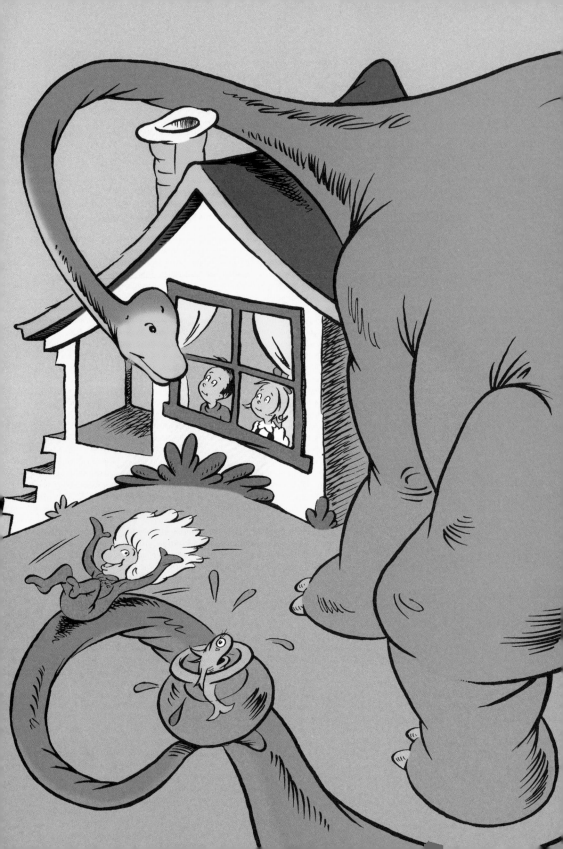

I'm the Cat in the Hat
(you have met me before).
Today I will speak
of the great dinosaur!

Dinosaurs lived
on the earth long ago,
before you and me.
So how do we know?

From fossils!
Dinosaur teeth, eggs, and bone
got stuck in the muck.
Then that muck turned to stone.

These fossils are old.
They are dusty and worn
because they were made
long before you were born.

Not hundreds of years,
not thousands of years,
but **millions** of years—
long before you were born!

Dinosaur hunters
dig in the ground.
All over the earth
these fossils are found.

The hunters use tools
to chip-chip all day.
The fossils come loose,
then they pack them away.

Fossils can crumble
because they are old,
so dinosaur hunters
must first make a mold.

To the dinosaur labs
every bone, tooth, and bit
is carefully shipped
to see how they fit.

Is this a leg bone?
Maybe a muzzle?
It's a crazy,
mixed-up
dinosaur
puzzle!

Step up and enter
the Museum Hall,
where dinosaurs stand.
Some are big.
Some are small.

Here we will play
the best of all games:
Oh Say Can You Say
the Dinosaurs' Names?

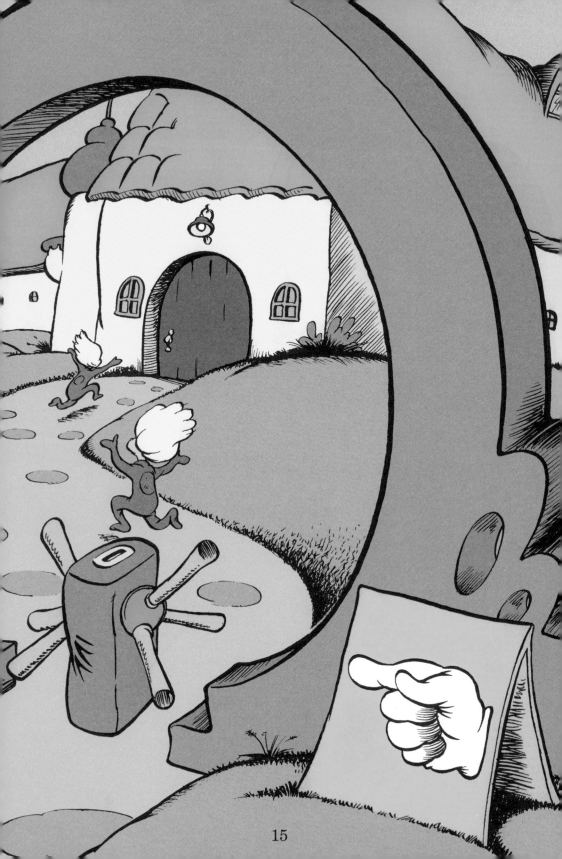

16

Take care of your father,
sweet Sally, dear Dick.
These long words can make
even grownups feel sick!

And after you've said 'em,
you then get to see 'em—
in the Cat in the Hat's
Super Dino Museum.

Dinosaur names
are not easy to read.
But give it a try.
(I will help if you need.)

Oh say can you say
ANG-
kih-
luh-
saw-
rus?
With a club for a tail
and a back full of spikes,
this dino was strong—
like an army tank. Yikes!

Now can you say
MY-
uh-
saw-
ruh?
There's one thing we know
that this dino did best.
She kept her kids cozy
and safe in their nest.

She kept the nest tidy.
She got her kids food.
She was a good mother
to her dino brood.

MAIASAURA

TYRANNOSAURUS REX

Now say
tie-
RAN-
uh-
saw-
rus
rex!
You said that quite nicely—
now you'd better go.
T. rex is no kitten,
I think you should know.